NOTE TO READER

Poe loves words—the bigger, the better. At the end of the book, you'll see a list of some of her favorites. As you read, try to guess which ones made the cut!

CONTRIBUTE A VERSE CREATIONS • HOUSTON, TEXAS

POE SCRUNCHED UNDER THE KITCHEN TABLE.

As was always the case when distressed, she sat, silently sniffing the worn nub of her lucky pencil eraser. It seemed to be the only thing that could calm her rattled nerves.

And as she sniffed, she pondered the source of her sorrows.

IT ALL BEGAN 8.452 YEARS AGO
ON THE DAY OF HER BIRTH.

ACCEPTABLE
UNACCEPTABLE

Her parents, two very well-meaning, but slightly kooky individuals, decided to name their first born "Poe"—due to their mutual adoration of poetry.

She would have much preferred Eleanor or Margaret or Elizabeth. They had way more syllables. No self-respecting scientist ever had a one-syllable moniker.

Despite her protest, her parents proceeded to decorate her bedroom with ponies and posies and the like until, at age 3.763, Poe called a family meeting and ordered the immediate cease and desist of all name-game word play.

When her little brother came along 2.137 years ago and was named “Alexander,” Poe nearly came unglued.

Four syllables and at least five noteworthy scientists and politicians for name-bragging rights?

To demonstrate her displeasure, Poe insisted on referring to him as “the dog.”

Today's particular trouble sprang from this name fiasco. You see, Poe was convinced that her name had somehow leaked its weird into the very fiber of her being.

She had always been a bit…different.

For example…

- Poe wore business suits—the Hillary Clinton variety—to school each and every day, accented by a bun coiled high and tight in an effort to appear more librarian-like.

- She thought a sensible pair of spectacles would take the look up a notch, but unfortunately, her eyesight was just about perfect. She had her mother buy old frames for her at the thrift store downtown and together, they poked out all the lenses so that Poe had a clear line of vision.

- On most days, Poe spent her recess reading the day-old *New York Times* that Principal Lawrence left in the recycling bin outside of his office.

You can imagine that Poe's proclivities led to some uncouth taunting on the playground. Pogo, Podo, Poo—simple and silly, yes—but an unkind word is an unkind word.

No matter how many syllables, it hurts just the same.

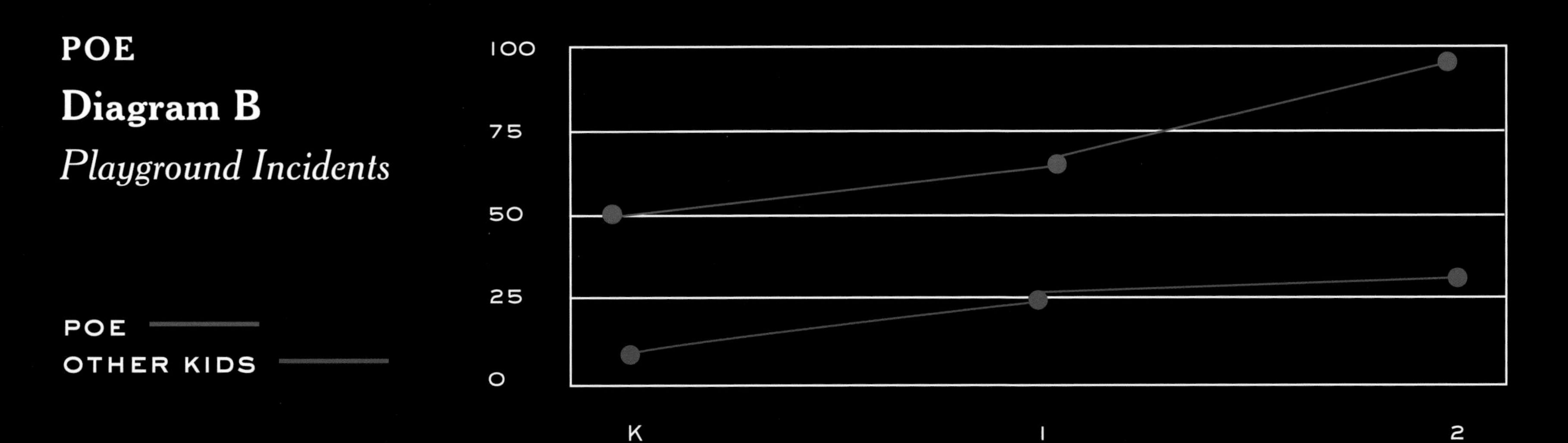

Now that you know a bit more about Poe, you may have a better idea of how this whole pencil sniffing incident began. That morning, Poe's teacher, Ms. Roe gave the class a writing assignment: "*The Most Important Thing…*"

Most of her classmates wrote paragraphs about their mothers. Not Poe. Inspired, she wrote 3.675 college ruled pages about pickle jars—her one and only obsession. When it was her turn to share, she didn't even make it through the first line before her class was in hysterics.

Poe was mortified… humiliated…irate. She didn't even get a chance to tell them about all the amazing things pickle jars can do.

LITTLE
SCIENTIST
MICROSCOPE

…they held the swamp water that she collected in the storm drains in front of her house when it rained. She spent hours bent over her "I'm a Little Scientist" microscope* examining the squiggling molecular creatures, convinced that one day, they would mutate and take over the world because of pesticide runoff and global warming.

**Just to clarify, she hated that name and had written to the manufacturer on several occasions to inform them that their product was ageist.*

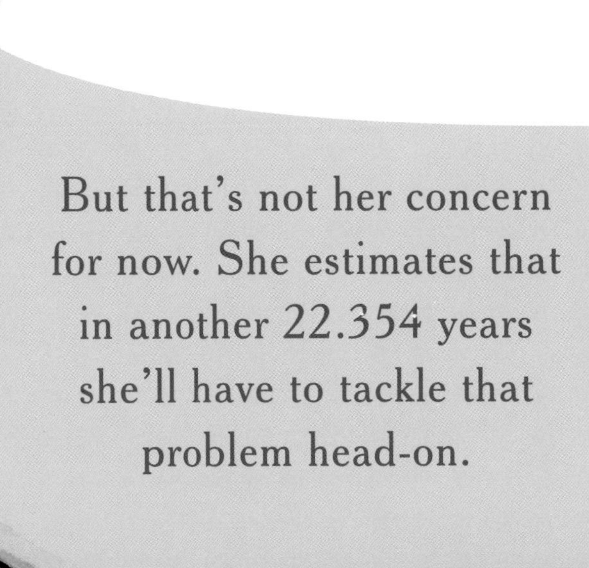

But that's not her concern for now. She estimates that in another 22.354 years she'll have to tackle that problem head-on.

…they were her holding tank of choice for the fireflies she caught in the summertime, several of which she *may* have sacrificed for a glow-in-the-dark art display on “the dog’s” face.

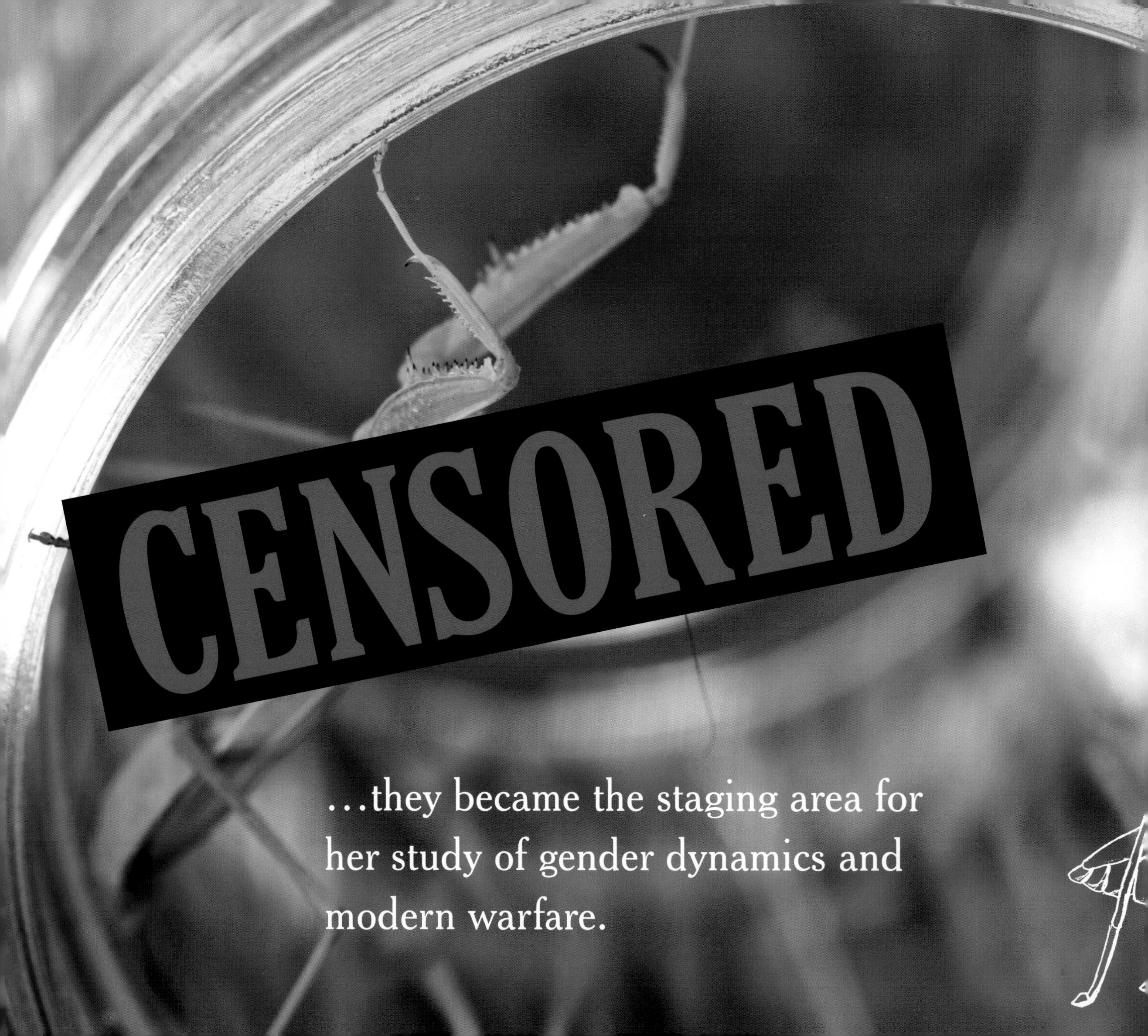

…they became the staging area for her study of gender dynamics and modern warfare.

She once caught two praying mantises
and placed them in the same jar—
purely for the sake of science of
course—and learned some painfully
honest lessons about love…and war.

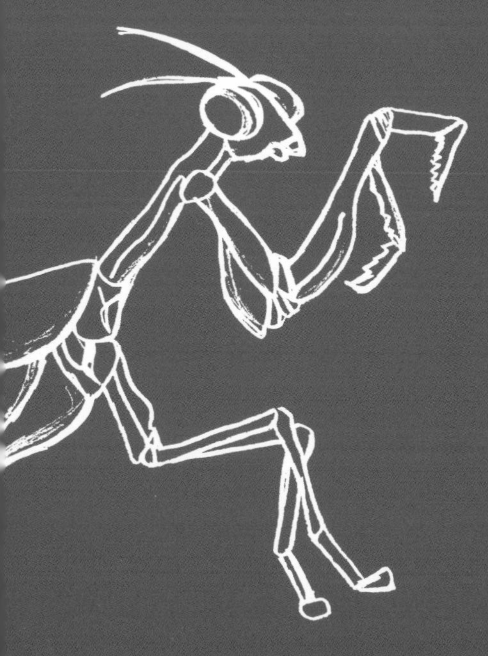

...they acted as storage for all of her collections.

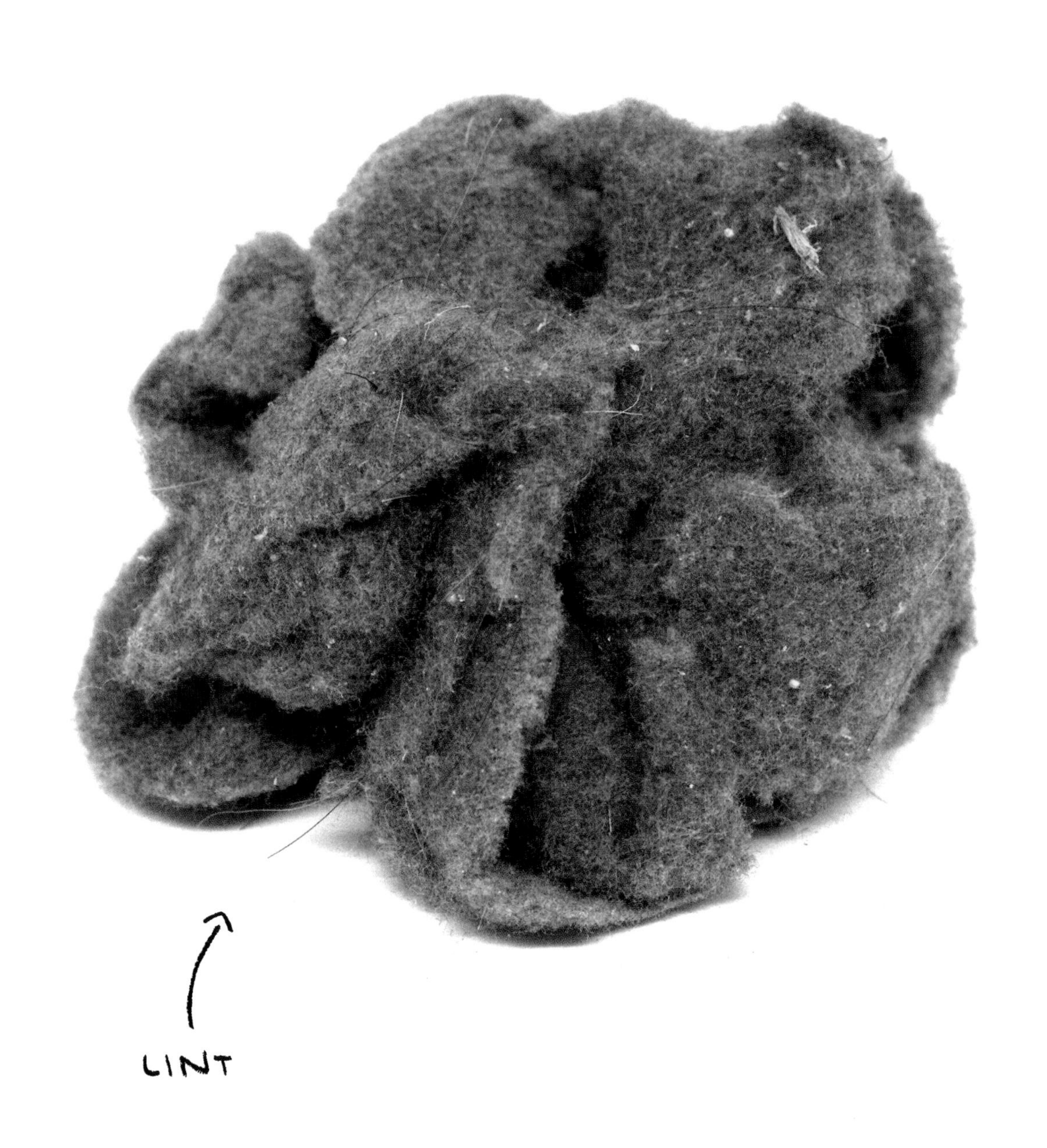

At that very moment, Poe had 48 pickle jars in her room containing an assortment of odds and ends, including:

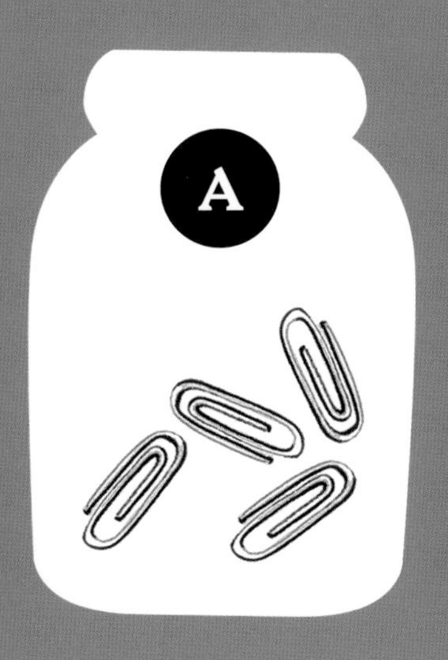

Paper clips and magnets

She was working on altering the Earth's magnetic field.

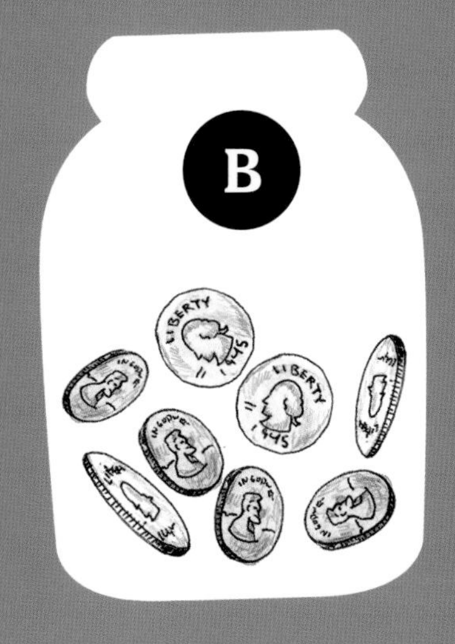

Spare change

She was saving up for a full set of encyclopedias for when the internet stops working.

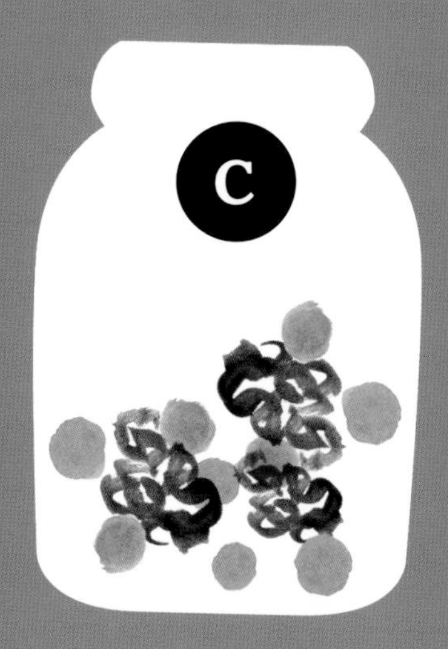

Dryer lint and slightly used bubble gum

She was conducting an experiment on how to eradicate child labor in textile mills world wide—it's a work in progress.

As you can see, Poe's passion for pickle jars was quite profound. She came home from school that day in tears—hence the pencil sniffing. But after a good talk with her mom and dad and some calming experiments on "the dog," all was well. Or so Poe thought…

The next morning, Poe entered the classroom to not-so-sweet smiles and not-so-whispery whispers of "Poe Pickles." She thought her new nickname a tad juvenile as "Poe the Peculiar" was technically more accurate and had way more syllables.

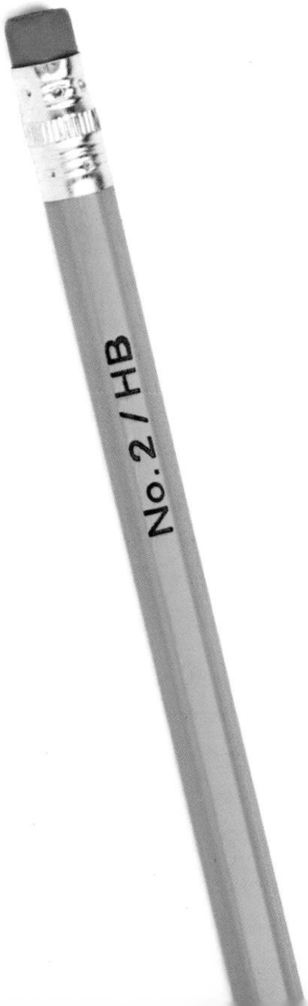

At recess, she was spreading her day-old copy of *The New York Times* beneath the slide in an effort to keep her newly dry-cleaned business suit neat, when she heard Ms. Roe call from the classroom door.

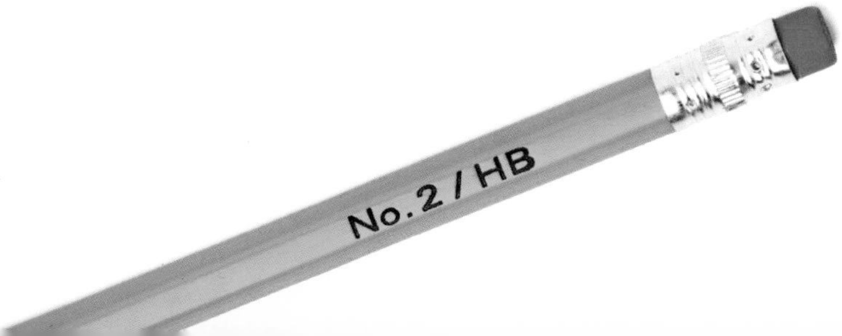

She folded her
newspaper carefully,
making sure not
to crease the latest
statistics on political
approval ratings,
and made her way
into the classroom—
head down,
eyes
full
of
tears.

Ms. Roe knelt down and took Poe's hands. "Poe," she said, "you and I have something in common, kiddo. Have you ever noticed how similar our names are?"

"Yes," Poe said, "they are both one syllable... and they rhyme...but I got stuck with a bad first name, at least yours is your last."

Ms. Roe smiled and looked not *at* Poe, but *into* her—into her very middle where all that hurt was making its home inside of her.

“That’s where you’re wrong, kiddo. My students call me by my first name.”

Poe looked up to see a secrety smile on Ms. Roe’s face.

Ms. Roe went on to tell her that her own mother had been a bit obsessed with Marilyn Monroe, and her insatiable quest for a life full of romance had inspired her to name her little girl after the very thing she so desperately sought.

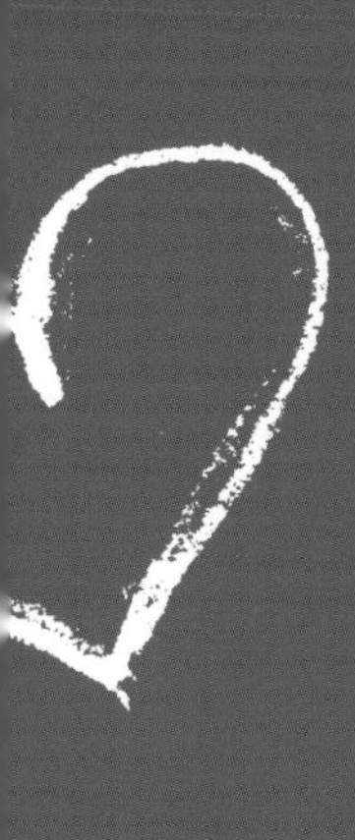

I was just like you, kiddo.

I felt like I was odd because of my name, and I thought that if I didn't let anyone get close to me, I wouldn't ever have to hurt. But hurt finds a way in anyway. I became mean because it was much easier to be mean than to be sad.

But one day, *my* teacher had a talk with me, just like I'm having a talk with you.

She saw a light in me—the very same light I see in you, Poe.

Those things that set you apart are the very things that make you a world-shaker!

When you walk out of this room, you get to make a choice.

You can hold that head up high, look through those specs and see yourself and the world around you in a brand new way, or you can sit under the slide on your *New York Times* and hurt.

You choose, kiddo."

Ms. Roe gave her a wink and stepped outside. Poe felt something inside her break. She cried a good cry and realized that her name didn't feel so heavy anymore.

On the way back to the playground, she heard the boy that sat behind her in class **SHOUT...**

"Hey, Poe Pickles, bet you can't hang from that top bar!"

Poe let down her bun and let her hair fly like her heart.

"That's *Ms.* Poe Pickles, thank you very much," Poe said, and she took his monkey bar bet.

She spent the rest of recess swinging upside down, looking at the world in a different way, and explaining the value of a pickle jar to the kids swinging all around her.

COPYRIGHT © 2016 CONTRIBUTE A VERSE CREATIONS
ALL RIGHTS RESERVED. THIS BOOK OR ANY PORTION THEREOF
MAY NOT BE REPRODUCED OR USED IN ANY MANNER WHATSOEVER
WITHOUT THE EXPRESS WRITTEN PERMISSION OF THE PUBLISHER
EXCEPT FOR THE USE OF BRIEF QUOTATIONS IN A BOOK REVIEW.

PRINTED IN THE UNITED STATES OF AMERICA

FIRST PRINTING, 2016

ISBN 978-0-692-68921-9

CONTRIBUTE A VERSE CREATIONS
HOUSTON, TEXAS

WWW.POEPICKLES.COM

PHOTOGRAPHY & ILLUSTRATION CREDITS
JOHN EARLES (ILLUSTRATIONS) Pickle Jars 1 & 13, Poe 2, 4, 6, Newspaper 8 & 20, Poe & Classmates 10-11, Poe & Pickle Jar 15, Pickle Jar Collection 19, Poe & Ms. Roe 22, Marilyn Monroe 24, Playground 30.

KELLY WINDHAM (PHOTOGRAPHY) Alexander 7 & 14, Poe 8, 12, 31, Poe & Kids on the Slide 14 & 28, Poe & Ms. Roe 24, 26-27.

ISTOCKPHOTO.COM (PHOTOGRAPHY) Tablecloth & Floor 2, 10-11, Dog 7, 14, Mantis 16, Pencil 21, Tissue 23.

DESIGN BY SPINDLETOP DESIGN